Wild

Sacred Erotica
Poetry

By Rachel Pringle

Wild Open

Wild Open

ISBN-13: 9781097335237

Wild Open

DEDICATION

I dedicate this book to the MUSE.
To the divine mystery that lives within all of us.
To the undeniable essence of creation that rests on her lips and urges
me to express freely and openly.
With you I expose my deepest heart
and my most transparent desires.
You are living, breathing permission.
I bow to you, the Divine.
The Maker that is HER.

ACKNOWLEDGMENTS

Deep gratitude for all the lovers in my life who
supported this creation.

To Yael Marantz, my sister wife, my guidance and undying support
throughout this entire process.
Thank you for everything you are.
Divine Feminine embodied.
All photos in this series are shot by Yael Marantz.

To my Mother for always being the wind beneath my wings, regardless
of how I choose to express.

To W and G for helping me unleash my hidden power.

And to my beloved husband, Johann.
You are the container in which I can explode over and over again. You
are my mirror, reflecting me so clearly so I can meet the deepest parts of
myself.
You love me like no other
and you free me like no other.
Thank you, I love you.

Wild Open

CONTENTS

FOREWORD

This book holds a message for you.
Through the evocations of the words within the pages of this book,
your spirit is invited into the present moment.
This poetry is for us. For us to be reminded of the melding and
merging of the sacred and slutty, of romance and raw primal desire,
of pain and pleasure, of the duality that resides inside of all of us.
To reveal and reconnect you with your erotic pulse.
I believe we are all desiring to express more potently and
profoundly than we ever thought possible.
We are yearning to expand past our boundaries and
experience ourselves completely and utterly ignited in every
aspect of our lives.
May these words liberate you.
May you witness your inner world come alive with the
knowing that there is more.
Dive fearlessly and indulgently into your true depths.
Stay a while.
Get to know these parts of yourself more intimately.
May these words give you the permission to claim your
right to pleasure.
Your pleasure is your access point to the divine force of all creation.
She takes all forms, she knows no bounds
and she doesn't discriminate.
All she wants is you to be YOU, FULLY.
May these words be that gift.
Read this once, Read this twice. Read this a million times.
It will always reveal more because it is a reflection of you.

Open

Into

DESIRE

FEEL

My being can sense his energy coming.
Leaving footprints in my mind as he walks with intention
up to the door.
Rising inside of me, as he pierces my thoughts, penetrating my soul.

Gently.

His eyes meet mine as I falter at the intensity of... him.
"Look at me", he says.

"Take me in".
I drink in his presence like a starved kitten lapping up milk.

I can't help but hide my face.

He holds my field and demands that I take him in.

"Look at all of me
Let me feel your body and soul inviting me in to you."

As my body slowly releases it's contraction I can feel his power trickle
into my cells.

A shiver erupts through my spine.

I'm scared to receive all of him yet his delivery wakes me.

"Take me." I beg.
And so he does.

LAY

I lay naked.
Naked body, naked soul, naked mind.

I lay ready.

I call him to me.
His consciousness touching the base of my spine.
Electricity. Glitter in my veins.
As my breath deepens so does his presence.
As he enraptures my senses, I open to him, unbound.
All that is clenched is now open.

I feel his consciousness entering me.

Sliding in and out. Without touch, I am completely taken.

My skin is heightened as I move my fingers up my thigh.
He removes all sense of control and pushes his way into my heart.
His tenderness is circular, moving around me, creating waves of energy
that leave me paralyzed in passion.
Pleasure present in every passing moment, slowly moving,
teasing me.

He knows I know.

He is here, watching me.

Watching me lose all control, desperate for his touch,
desperate for the soul of him unleashed.

VISION

You are a vision.

Electric wild spirit.

Invade my soul and let me swim in your power.
I try to run away, but you always catch me.
With patience you destroy my barriers.
My boundaries disappear.
My hunger for you dominates my every move.

I want to express into you.

Blow creation into your open heart.

Creep into your thoughts and envelope you with my
essence.
Push my body into yours as I leave bite marks along your neck.

Tear you apart and put you back together.

Pleading for you to destroy me with your presence.

You absorb my wet openness as I release a delicate cry of desire.

Exploding with lust, I lavish in your unending fury.

Blown wide open.

BLUR

I am in-prisoned by your energetic draw.

You call me in so sweet, so nasty.

You wait and tease me tenderly until I am fully enveloped in your arms.

Our roots intertwine together in a rhythmic dance of lust,
I am floored by how your energy charges mine.

I feel you in each cell, drawing blood, knocking down
barriers and filling me up with the desire to expand past my fears.

My skin talks to me, yearns for me to melt into yours and bathe my
body in your sweet nectar.

As I take you, tongue licking your salty skin, my mouth is
electrified with a desire to consume you.

To taste your cock.
To know what the union of my womb pressed into you is like.
You fill me, floor me, ignite my whole cunt to attention.

I beg you to never stop.
Pressing into me, so gentle with your awakened presence.
You walk all over my lines and blur my sense of reality.
Allowing me to fall away from the stories that run wild in my mind.
Simply existing in the undying pleasure of our freedom.

TIGHTER

His hand streams into my hair.
Pulling it tightly, just enough that I want him to do it more.

More. More. More.

I close my eyes and lean my head back.

He is grasping my presence with his hands.

Allowing me to surrender to his influence over me.
I squirm when his breath touches my neck.

Hot heat grazing my curves, affecting me, opening me.
Saturated fully, my body, my pussy, welcomes him.

His teeth imprinted on my skin.

He is gentle yet impossibly firm

He wants me to know who is in control and I submit to him.

Feeling his love crack me open to receive.

Wild Open

Discover

Your

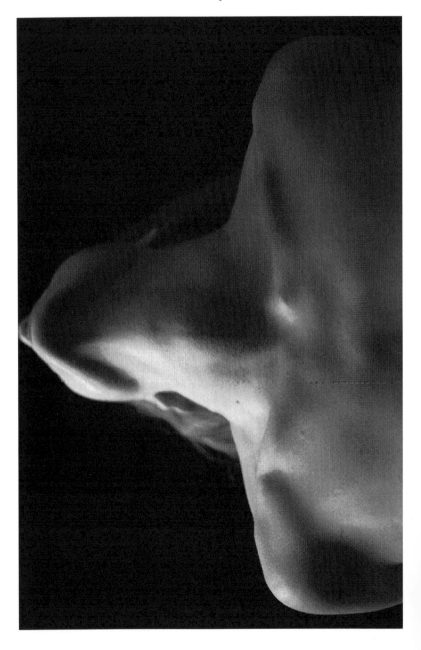

RAW

GENTLE

His hands slip into my hair.
Caressing my skin so gently.

He loves me.

Clasping my hand in his.
His power elevates me.
He invades my thoughts with purity, with lust.
He unwinds me as I expand into him, tracing my curves with
remembrance.

Licking my ankles as I scream.

He loves teasing me, punishing me with unending rapture.
Demolishing my every fear and disappearing into my soul,
to lick me clean from the inside.

His eyes never leave mine.
He watches me tremble, basking in my vulnerability.
He seeks me utterly exposed.

So he can pour himself into me.
So we are no longer separate.
So my pain turns into pleasure.
So I am undressed of every past burn, meeting him in the pure erotic
sin of our union.

I am his.

CHARGED

I am charged by your exhalation.

I can feel you all over me.

Desperate for the union of my heart and yours,
of my root and yours.

Of you climbing up my spine with your snake and spinning my chakras
into oblivion.

I bow down to your power as you succumb to mine.
I gasp at the realization of your thought stream entering mine.
Visceral memory of you pressing into me.

Fuck me.
Fuck me open.
Fuck my skin so it can finally be free of the old stories and ways
I used to be.

Touch me.
Touch me in every way.

I'll follow you into the deep darkness, swim in the black flames,
be there to cry into your open mouth as we merge to meet our
deepest truth.

UNBOUND

Open the door. Look at me.
Strip me down. Look at me.
Lay me down.
I'm nervous.
I'm nervous of you seeing me yet I want to give you everything.
Rip it off. Rip off the shame of you seeing me.
See me fully.
My soul is weeping as you watch me.
My body is carnal. Alive for the first time.
Asking you to take me fully.
You seduce me with your being, with your body.
You inch towards me as I begin to shake, gently caressing me.

I beg for you.

You seem so calm. It makes me wet. My raw awakens.
I am unbound as you lay your skin on mine.
Pressing your lips to mine.
Enveloping my mouth with yours.
Your tongue invites my erotic memory to the surface.
I remember what it's like to be an animal.
Wild nature, ready to pounce.
To prey on you like you are my sustenance.
Because you are. You know that you are.
Take me deeper.
Let me bask in the splendor of my body at full attention.
You devour my heart with your presence as I submit my
everything to you.

As you honor my soul so fully by showing me yours.

AWAKE

As I lie awake in your arms I feel you open to me.
I feel you merging with the parts of me that quiver in pain.
You stare deep into my eyes.
The wonderment of you opening my healing with your love breaks me
down into tears.
You use my tears as lubrication to unwind my tension and graze my
skin with your fingertips.
Tightly you embrace my hips with your hands.
Pressing your thumbs deeply into me as I squirm.
You see me so purely and my heart aches to be met by you.

By your pleasure.

You invade my deepest parts.
Spreading yourself all over me.

Bringing your tongue to my sensitive crease.
Licking me open until I let go of all fear.
As you stare longingly, lovingly into my eyes and drive your sweet fin-
gers into my cunt I collapse around you.
I allow you to hear all my moans and screams with complete abandon.
I no longer hold back as I receive your cock, into my sacred pussy,
up my spine, penetrating my heart with your consciousness.

Feeling the snake of your existence licking my third eye.
I relinquish all control.
Exploding with primal fury, knowing that I am safe
with-in me, within you.
Melting into you.
Embracing my majesty with your every thrust.

BEING

As your eyes bear into mine, I am seeing into your soul.
You are an animal.
Fast, strong, baring teeth, wanting to devour.
No need to be polite or proper, you show me who you are and
I open to you.
I succumb to your pheromones and beg you to rip away
my barriers, my fear, my shy nature and return me to the place of
complete liberation.
Raw, naked and wet.
I want you, I want all of you to take me.
To take all of me.
To see me in my most vulnerable places and press your
mindfulness deep inside of me.
I can feel you crawl into my skin and kiss every layer of my being.
Dripping your essence into my cells and fucking my pain body with
your patience and presence.
You recognize my beauty, reflect it back to me in your breath.

Slow, deep, full.
You calm me down, slow me down, take me down to the core of
existence where the earth generates warmth and radiates life
into everything.
Meeting my aura with yours.
As our energy spins in unison,
I feel the dizziness of complete surrender.
The letting go of all old lovers who never saw me.
Finally meeting myself as you hold the space for my greatest unraveling.

Elicit

Your

WILD

WET

My senses are disturbed at the appearance of his name.
The nectar is alive, dripping down.
Peeling me back, drawing him forward.
He looks deeply into me.
Immediately I release tears of exposure.
He lays me down, beginning to lick my tears.
I am paralyzed with the desire to be possessed.

Undress me.
With your eyes and your hands.
Dive deep into my divine.
He is the volcano, alive inside me.
Rapid, yet steady, he breaks me open.

He looks at me. Into me. Through me, And to me.

Gently he slides his middle finger inside of me.
Calling me forward.

So tight, so open.

Never leaving my eyes, his lips beckoning me to receive him.

The breath streams out of my open mouth.
The sound so silent it penetrates the space, so loud.

He breathes my breath in and we fade into union.

FEEL

I can feel you coming before you even enter the room.
I can feel your energy brimming against mine
as you walk up the stairs.
I can feel you infiltrate my system with your sacred essence,
flooding my loins with hot, wet heat.
As your eyes meet mine there is an inner knowing.
An understanding that I am yours.
You claim me as yours and you will destroy anything that keeps
you from me.
The lust I feel is beyond all depths.
It rises in my toes and electrifies my inner thighs as I sense your
tongue dying to touch my lips.
You are still looking at me.
You haven't even touched me, yet I feel you all over me.
As I lean back completely taken by you,
I can finally feel your hot exhale on my neck.
Everything is erect within me, including you.
As you part my legs open and brush your palm against me,
my body seethes with fire.
Fuck me now.
Press yourself inside me and let me merge with your awareness.
Yet you continue to tease me, grabbing my neck.
Holding me so tightly that I can let my whole being go.
You play with my energy and push me beyond my limits.
Finally taking my neck into your mouth and gliding your tongue down
my breasts.

I am yours.
Unabashedly I give myself to you. Wild nature appearing,
returning as my body awakens to my carnal needs.

WILD

Wild soft eyes gaze back at me.
His stare is laced with primal fury.
Dismantle me, I beg.

Rip apart everything you see and drink me in.
Taste me.
Merge with my aroma.
Relish in my sweet scent.

The intensity lingering on his fingertips, inching towards me.
Pleasure center purring.
Come closer I urge.
Savor my love as it drips into your mouth.
He consumes me.
Opening me like a flower, tracing every petal.
Inviting me to relinquish everything to him.
As I spread myself bare.
He takes me in. He takes me deep inside his mouth.

Alive in exposure. I share my secrets with him.

My burning pain diminishing as he sets my body ablaze.
Stripping away all of who I've never been.

He sees me.
He is seeing me.

Seeing me rise, open and fade into a blissful surrender.
Piecing me together with his passion.

AURA

I want to bathe in your aura.

Consume every particle of you.

Drink all of the air surrounding you.
Basking in your balmy scent, I devour your essence.

So sweet. So naughty.

My animal is awake.
Furious for your wild.
Bend me over. Strip me down.

Licking my thighs, my skin becomes dangerously alive.
I'll break you.
Destroy you with my love.
Flow into your every wound, pouring divinity into your darkness.

Fuse together our every desire and split your center.

Enter you here.

Infiltrate your being and breathe myself into you.
Drowning you in the velvet of my mind.

I float your presence to the top.
Meet me here.

Allow me to see you.

PIT

In the pit of my stomach I ache for you.

My heart bleeds as I think of you.

Remember me, don't ever forget me.
My smell, my untethered essence provoking you to take me.
Grazing my thigh, igniting my unbound nature.

I am wild, your wild.

You unleashed me, you unleash me.

Lick away my tears as I cum for you.
As I cum to remember who I really am.
Lock eyes with mine, stare into me, sync your breath with mine.

Feel me feeling you.
Stroking our magnetic fields.
Heightened, so close yet so far.

I feel you.
I feel you feeling me.

Our secret territory where we are left bare, raw and uncovered.
Bathing in each other's cosmic release, of pure love.

Dissolve

Into

ENRAPTURE

LIPS

His fingers linger on my knee.
How could someone's touch envelop me entirely?
He peers into me, eyes open so wide.
He is untamed.

He wants me feral.

He wants to play with my path to heaven.
Tormenting me until I plead for him to put his lips to mine.

I am fiending, desperate for more.

For full immersion into his crude delicious touch.
Whispering into my mouth.
His tongue touches mine and my body convulses.
Take me.

Never stop

Not until you decimate my every thought and I erupt into the
satisfaction of your power entering my holy space.

AROUSAL

As soon as his foot hits the floor I feel the heat rise.
His eyes meet mine and my body is fully erect.

I drink him in.

Slurping, watching, waiting.
I allow my energy to permeate him.
He fixates on me. Watching me intently.
I open my legs for him.
As I lick my finger, his mouth falls agape.

My gaze never leaves his.

I plead with him to touch me.

His presence, so pure, makes my body scream for him.
He moves like a lion after his prey, resting his hand on my thigh, showing me his dominance.
Flood gates pour open as he glides and rides my skin with the base of his palm.
He is my maker, he owns my pleasure.

He owns me because he knows I am only owned by myself.

He sees my freedom and demands more.
I succumb to his every movement, burying my passion into his heart.
He opens, submitting himself to the divine, disappearing into ecstasy.

ADDICT

The addictive nature of your succulent skin.
The way you desire my flesh against yours.
It's sinful how good you taste in my mind, how electrified I am at the sight of you undressing.
Arousal seeks me constantly as I evoke your wildest wishes with the sway of my hips.
I pierce through your brain, enter your third eye, lubricate your mind with the meditation of our vessels converging.
Synced and surrendered into the holy trinity with spirit.

Fuck me, I pray.

Spread me thickly all over your being.

Get on your knees to beckon the goddess within.
She is your muse and I am her maker.
She is the creator of your wettest dreams, making you crawl to her feet, drinking her sacred cum.
My toes curl, the pressure of you leaning your way into me.
I never imagined a man could create storms of pleasure inside my every thought.
Drip, drop, drawl, saunter your way into me, make me yours.
I long to bathe in the texture of your name in my mind.
The vibration of your breath on my ear.

You and only you can make me beg in this way.

Beg for the presence of a man fully empowered.

BIRTH

The exasperation of needing you.
I need you to penetrate me.
My heart, my soul, my pussy.
Enter me with your wakefulness,
erect your consciousness into my being.
Sharply you command my attention, wrenching the
mundane out of my experience.
Lacing your every movement with depth and purity.

I want you to own me, open me to God.
Take your fullness and enter every part of me that hurts.

Lick my dryness, lubricate my soul with your wild untamed nature.
You devour me whole and still I beg for more.
Take me, claim me, penetrate me with your tender loving and drip
ecstasy all over my body.
You devil of a man, you betray all stereotypes and leave light in their
wake.

You tear away the film of filth to reveal my opulent temple.

You bow to the ripples of my skin, kiss the curves of my body like I am
the living, breathing goddess of the underworld.

You, you, you, show me, me.

You relinquish control so I can dominate your field with my
animalistic ways and give birth to the existence
of our love unbound.

CUNT

Nasty delicious cunt.

Drown me now in your endless fluid.
Bury me in your sweet nature and pour the gasoline of your
fire all over me.
Set me aflame so I never remember anyone else's name.

Fuck me open.

Something so raw.
Scream for Shiva.
Allow yourself to perish underneath my desire.
Let me delve into your soul and kiss the inner workings of the goddess.
Heal your wounds and let you be the glorious mess of love
completely unwound.

Free.

Free of you, free of me.

Beneath all else we remain.

No longer separate but united in the divinity of our pleasure.

Meet

The

PRESENCE

YOURS

I can taste your skin.

Feel your eyes as you long for me.
I can feel you search for me.
Erect pressure rising inside you.

You can't help but think of me in every moment.

Trace my sweat with your tongue.
Tear my skin away and kiss my insides.
I surrender to the depth of your being.

I crush your fear with my love.

Swallow your wounds, painting tender glory over your every cell.
As I whisper to your inner most child I feel you open to me.
As you open I become moist with the grace of your presence.

I relish in the splendor of your sacred masculine heart and spray my
fiery fury all over your patient face.
Show me yours and I'll show you mine.
Forever unraveling your danger, spreading your heart open and re-
awakening my rage.
Sharing with you the sweetest taste of my cunt alive.

I long for you and only you.

TEASE

Tease me tenderly as my skin ripples open to your breath.
I bow in worship to the pleasure of my opening.

You seeing into me.

Breaking past all my barriers as I unravel in front of you.
I am ablaze, burning from the core.
You lick my skin, soothing my insides with your
magnificent demeanor.

Everything is ok.

I am enlivened with you.

I escape the terror of mediocre presence and blast fully open into the
being-ness of my existence.

Laden in glory and richness.

You weave your essence into the fabric of my being and whisper God's
permission into my ear.

SATURATE

Make a hole in my body with your finger.
Slide in and take what's yours.

Claim me.

Pleasure me forever as I make love to your heart and show you real
healing.

I will puncture your mind.

Unravel old, delinquent stories, forcing you to remember your undying
spirit as you meet me in the cosmic wave.
Pray to my womb as we open portals to new dimensions,
surrendering to the love we are so scared of.

You are me, I am you. We are one.

Pretending to be separate and feeling the draw of our loins in union.
Vibrating in pure magic as it ripples through our veins,
asking our sensory nature to be alive once again.
To remember the colors of prisms illuminating the
existence of the divine.

I long for you to meet me here.

The secret passageway into heaven through our undying touch.

HOLD ME

Hold me as I release my every thought, melting into you.
Only now, only here.

Safe.

I am safe here.

To disappear completely into the mystery.
Dancing with the fear, with the unknown.

No longer scared.

You make me remember the strength within me.
You carry my heart in yours.

You play my love strings with your consciousness and
create the melodies of the universe.
The rhythm of us is majestic, yet simple like a wildflower.

Unhinged, present.

I imagine a life where you enter my soul with every breath,
realizing that it is now.

If only I can see you are here and so am I.

And that is all I've ever needed.

TEMPLATE

The delicious understanding of you filling my body with your template
of consciousness.
Making my whole pussy drip with God's saliva as you
tenderly stroke my being with your fingertips.

You make it look so easy, yet I travel with you through waves of the
deepest emotions.

You want to know my truth so deeply you engorge yourself on my sacred flesh and enrapture your mind with my genius.

Drinking in my moans and vibrations with an open mouth and a
never ending heart.

I will forever bask in this fury of the unknown.
The darkness of the black hole of your mind,
your willingness to test and taste every ounce of me, and you.

Bury yourself inside me to feel the full union of our serpents
eating one another.
Swallowing me whole, only to meet me again.

Desiring to know my expanded self with every kiss.
Seeing into my eyes so defiantly,
I disintegrate into the mysterious waters of our primal appetite.

Surrender

To

HER

SILK

Silk dark hair falling into my mouth.
I remember your gaze as you peered into me.
I rest in the unrest of your glare.

You want me.
No matter how unsafe it may be, you travel into the realm to find me.
You are slick like grease working your way through my
being, through my body, to deliver your remedy,
your medicine, of pleasure.
Whisper into my pussy with your sweet melodic ways.

As I tremble you become aware that your presence moves me.

You opening.

Me withering, wet with yearning.

Remembering that I am allowed to feel you.
Magnetic waves invade my worries, gather them up like
kindling to set a blaze.

No more fear.

I am yours now, I relax into your delicate warmth, feeling your field
merge with mine.

RIPPLES

She ripples through me.
Her elegance finds it's way inside of my heart, into my veins.

I watch her mouth as she speaks to me.

The curves of her lips like mountains I want to climb over and over again.

As she whispers in my ear I am shocked by my desire to penetrate her, to be penetrated by her.

I feel her dripping all over me.
Rippling with desire to taste me.
For me to kiss the valley of her neck, inviting her most naughty nature to come alive.

"I see you," she says.

"You are safe to open me. I want to worship you. Worship the parts of you that other women shamed. I want to heal your wounds with my honey loving."

Tenderly she waits for me as I realize I can fall into her.

I can release my every thought, swim into her cosmic wave, riding this unknown journey into the heavens.

THREE

Oh the unearthly joy of experiencing your minds drifting into mine.
I want to watch you fuck.

I want to pleasure my whole body at the image of you thrusting your
consciousness into her.
Witnessing you, watching me, watching you.
You both dripping with each others pure fluids, bathing in the rarity of
our togetherness.
My loins run so hot, yearning for the patience of our
energies melting, melding, merging.
I never imagined I'd be so simply satisfied with the thoughts coming
alive in my mind.
Fucking in my mind.

You, her, me.

Opening me, by opening her.
Opening her, by trusting me.

Thrusting your devotion and commitment deep into the
passageway of her heart, reminding her that you'll never leave.

By knowing me you are simply knowing deeper into her.

I relish in witnessing you, feeling the union of our souls bathed in erotic
exposure.

The willingness to let the thoughts be worn as clothes only to be ripped
off in the fury of our naked truth.

GRAZE

My flower drips open as you stare at me with those curved eyes.

Soft gentle gaze makes me feel wet with ease and opening.
I feel your fingertips graze my skin, sending shock waves of the highest
delight deep inside my pussy.

I'm scared to feel this way about you.

Your illuminating radiance so alarmingly forceful.
Without even knowing you've already made your way into my heart.
Graceful brilliance sweeping your hair up and down my body.

Tasting your tongue on mine.

Moaning at the deliciousness of your pale skin yearning
to be eaten.
You enter my dreams with creamy waves of our souls stroking
one another.
Of your mouth kissing the heart of my flower,
awakening the universe that lies within it.

You welcome my nectar, invite me to meet your presence.
Your embodied movement takes me deeper into a potent trance of
Cleopatra.

Hunger.
Pure lust and deep love, the merging of hearts and skin.
The opening of your energy in mine.

Express

Your

DEVOTION

DARK

Take me to the underworld I begged.

The vast place of destruction.

Where I can meet my rage with the fury of your compassion.
Loving every inch of the darkness that once failed me.
You remind me over and over again of the beauty of who I truly am.
You pleasure my shame with your ownership over my presence.
You stand so strong, so solid that no matter how erratic I feel you hold my every tear.
You open my sacral with your piercing presence, pouring your love into my unconscious.
You bring light into the realms less traveled, nurturing the grounds of my deepest heart.

You flower my being with your hands on my face, your words soothing my mind.
You accept me, open me, relieve me from the chaos of this maze of abandonment and betrayal.
You show yourself so fully that I surrender my every cell into the home of your heart.
You disappear my pain by seeing me fully.
Never turning away.
You ignite my being with your potent truth.
With your allowance for everything to be seen,
the transparency of our aching souls being replenished by the dance of our patience and depth.

WAVES

Iridescent waves of your naughty ways.

You fly right by me, circling my head, sinking your stinger in my skin,
forcing me to attention.
I disappear, falling deeper in love with my wholeness
through your eyes.

I cherish your heart beating into mine,
your legs intertwining with mine.
Your sacred energy brushing against mine,
stillness as you place your hand over mine.

You cradle my head with your palm while fucking god into
every particle of my existence.

The pleasure eradicates my senses and so I am filled by the
presence of space.

Of the nothingness that is mystery.

The unknown of my pleasure that is buried in pain yet steeped in un-
ending ecstasy once released.

You take the time to dig deep into my crevices, opening me like the
wildflower that I am.

You watch me as I blossom for you.
Betroth my pussy as your guide to the cosmos,
writing poetry with your tongue upon my skin.

SHIVA

Your eyes are lit with fury.
I can feel your attention as you desire to obliterate my boundaries with
your love.
No pain without pleasure first.
Open me, expand me.
Awaken my skin as you lick my whole body alive.
Spank me, grope me, make me feel like the sacred slut I truly am.

Fondle my cosmic cunt.

De-armor all my pain as you fill my being with your
otherworldly heavenly dominance.
Tracing my insides as you discover every pathway.
The gateways worth caressing, the places once forgotten.
You fill my every worry with a presence of pure divinity.
You balance my complete chaos with the undying
remembrance of my true spirit reflected back to me in your eyes.

Look at me.
Fuck me open, Shiva.

Take me to the place of no return.
Banish my every thought of separation as we blast into
each others' soul.
Lick my tears as I surrender to my greatness, witnessing you in
devotion to me.

ABYSS

Tightly wound.

As he enters the room his breath opens me, enters my skin.
My body, my being, begin to pulse.
Secreting my scent, my fragrance of divinity.
I am calling him forward.
Lick me, enter me, marry my pain with your pleasure and wrap your
tongue around my heart.

Beating heart.
Faster, faster.

As I drip down my thigh I yearn for him.

I am the opening.

Enter me, penetrate me with your consciousness.
Bathe me in your presence, painting my body with your breath.
In this moment I will know the glory of my being open to God.
To the Goddess rising in me, watching you, seeing me, meet her.

Basking in the way you bow to me.

I envelop her as she intertwines with me.
I open my cosmic cunt for you to meet the space of
darkness and stars.
Die, into me and I will meet you where the unknown is the
greatest pleasure.

CONTAINER

As I disappear into your scared container I face my fears with depth.

I own me. I own the awareness that I am your mirror.

It is my duty to bear witness to your consciousness,
bleeding truth into your heart in the most profound tones.

To let my pussy rule your presence and curate your life.

To show you who you are.

To drip my soul nectar into your mouth and guide you to the truest
expression of you.

The intricate knowing that I dominate your heart with my fluid like
lips, pouring my pleasure into you.

Fingering your heart, Un-raveling all the ropes and
destroying your every sour thought of the female form.

I bathe you with my undying softness, graciously tongue your beautiful
face and lick your eyes open to your truth of our togetherness.

Experience

Your

DIVINITY

BITE

How deeply I covet for our cells to dance the eternal dance of pleasure.

I want you to break me open so wide that I tremble at the fact that you could kill me.

Break me open to the wildness that resides inside my erotic lips.

Destroy my every barrier that keeps me from expressing the unknown madness of my deepest desires.
Bite my face and demand that I run free.
Hold me safe as I release Amrita to flow like the most beautiful river, you creating my forever river bank.

As you hold me I fall open to my divination unbound.

Desperately seeking to know my fullest expression you push your wand to wake the rage of my eternal fire, finally unleashed.

I completely unravel into the beauty of your existence witnessing mine.
We merge as one, floating in a pool of lovers thoughts.

DIVINE

This union, unified and united.
Together we melt into one, into three, into the beginning,
the precipice of the fall.
We birth each other again and again.
Seeding me with your wicked ways, begging me to spray you with my
holy waters.
Eyes gazing into endless passage ways.

It's never ending with you.

With your tongue stroking mine, gripping my neck in
endless desire to make me yours.
My skin stands at attention as your heart opens to me.
The glory of your heart seeping into mine is my greatest desire.

Fuck me with your open heart.

Rub the blood of your joy all over my being and let me drink the pleasure of your commitment.

You committed to seeing yourself in my mirror.

I clean myself for you.
Clean all my shame and guilt away so you can see your self and reflect
me back.
I worship the presence of your undying love looking at me.
I see your Adonis body, devoting myself to your rawest realest pleasure
of being seen and adored so fully.
I drink you in, overflowing my divinity into yours.
Together we are one.

GOLDEN LIGHT

This disappearance of our spirits meeting in oblivion.
Tasting our sacred tears to unite and transmute our fears,
charging forth into an alternate dimension.

I open my vessel to feel your divine sword slay all my illusions.

Lay my being back to rest in the realm of no separation.
Where I can always hear the whisper of my truth upon your tongue,
reminding me that I am one.

With you, With me, With thee.

With the essence of this pleasure of protection that only I possess from
within my soul.

I am the maker and you the serenader of my creations back into me.
Wrapping my limbs in golden light, lifting my heart into flight with
your laughter.
Your ease even when I'm drowning in my sorrow is my ticket to the
gateways of heaven, my own truth.

The womb of my own awakening.

Where I can meet you.
And yet you remind me again and again that only I can take me there.

SPACE

I remember myself through you.
It takes patience to see myself so clearly, to see all that I am laid before me.
For you to open up your bare arms, present your chest full of hair in all the right places, enveloping me in your subtle scent of days of purpose.
Safe.
A part of me hates that you know me so well, yet I relish in the fact that I unwind my whole soul as you witness me.

To feel you is to feel me.

You push me, break me, open me beyond what I can
handle on my own.

You sear so deeply into my realm with your words and
penetrating stare.
I melt at the becoming of your power as mine.

I am no different than you.
You are me, I am you, we are we and I am true, when I look at you.
When I challenge you, I channel you, the divine in you.
Overflow love into you, to remind you, of your truth.

I recognize my purpose when I breathe deeply into you.
Facing my godliness no matter how many times I try to ignore it, to
forget it.

There you are.
Reminding me.

MIRROR

I look at you lovingly.
I want to comfort you, to take your pain away.
I am your mirror.

I have a duty to shine my expression into your soul in way that doesn't
feel safe to me.
In a way that disintegrates my old identity, raising me into a
deliverance and resilience that shocks your system open to me.
That tricks all your barriers, unlocks your vaults, opening you to me.
I ground myself deep in my intuitive waters to serve you
at your highest.
I will bow to you, bow to your cock and suck you off like I'm at God's
throne, because I am.
I worship the part of you that is infinite.
The part of you that seeps with power and I will devour you in my
mouth to remind you of your duty here.
To be the presence of God in every moment.
To open others to their godliness, allowing your essence to
penetrate their soul in a way that brings awareness of the
most potent form.
Bringing you down to your knees in praise of my delivering you your
remembering.
Surrender to the snake that dissolves all your armor,
opening you to the heart of all hearts.
To the pleasure of being fully seen even in the midst of your anger.
To open my throat, taking you in so you can feel the power of my cause.
Where your wounds can be met with light,
bathing in the fullness of my love.

Meet

The

BELOVED

YOU

I am ashamed to say that I don't know who I am without you.
Without your loving embrace, your quiet stillness to hold my wild nature.
Your patience as I paint out stories of lovers scorn,
wounds left open and battered.

I return to who I am when I am with you.

You hold the mirror so clear I have no choice but to see and face my brilliance.
To let go of the foolish story I hold and see straight into the divine.
To relish in the glory of my un-ending ability to breathe life into everything that I do.

You remind me the shame I see is illusion.
The judgment I face is my dearest friend whom merely needs my love and attention.

"It is ok to love and want me," he says.
Because I am you in the purest form and you are me in cosmic intervention.
We mirror each other back to the source of our greatest remembering.

Opening to the truth of no return.

We are one.

We have never been apart.

You love me so because I remind you of home.

The place that your every cell reads and feels is electric.

Re-emerging with the omnipresence that we give one
another over and over again.
The laughter of licking each others wounds,
of bearing each others pain.

"You never blame me," he says.

You only look to me to remind you.
How could there be any greater gift than to remind the
divine that she is so.
To swim in your grace, in your purity, drinking the
nectar that is your love.

I bow to you simply because in so I am bowing to me.

To us, to we, to THEE.

To the wild, untethered nature of our beings running free,
like children of existence that know no end and no beginning.

Open

About The Author

Rachel Pringle is an artist and leader in women's empowerment. She has been immersed in the study of human development and the mysteries of the mind, body and soul for over two decades.

She is committed to the subtleties and intricacies of unraveling the self that led to opening and healing the physical body, allowing for true ownership of our unique essence.

This is her first book of poetry. This body of work was created out of major heartache and loss of self. Through the devotional act of claiming Her
sovereignty, she began a creative process that led her to access a channel of erotic awakening that has and continues to profoundly change her life. By sharing the art that was birthed from her pain, her desire is to inspire others to access their power.

WWW.IAMRACHELPRINGLE.COM
@PositivePringle

Printed in Great Britain
by Amazon

14182198R00059